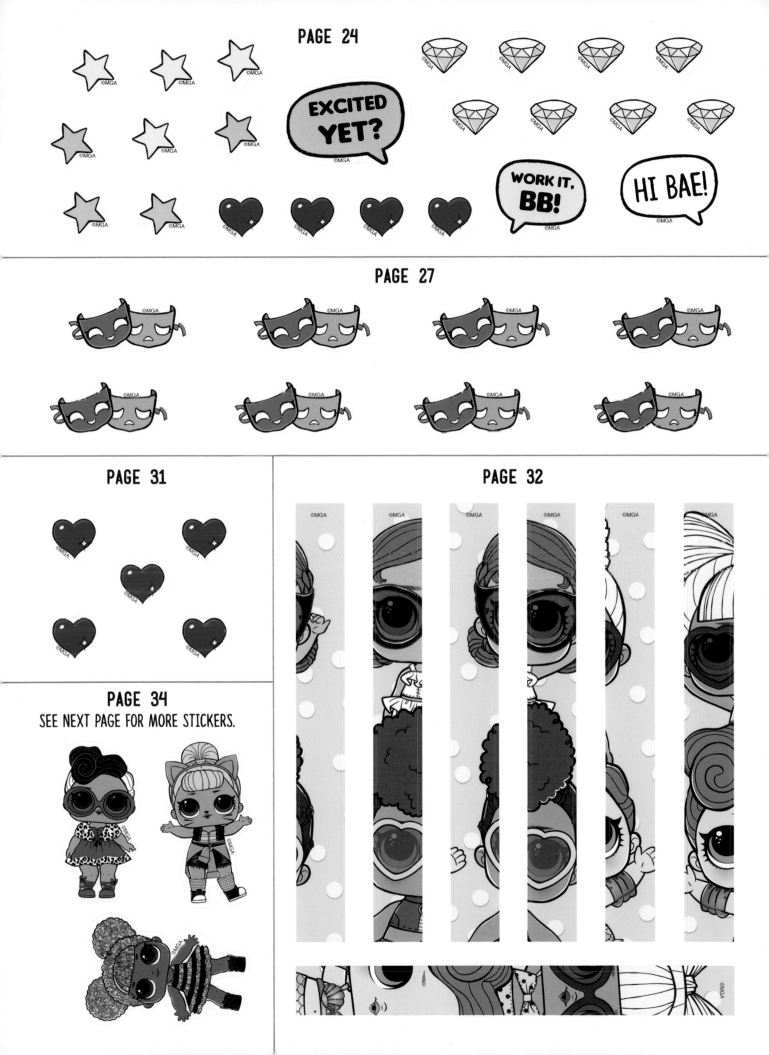

PAGE 24

EXCITED YET?

WORK IT, BB!

HI BAE!

PAGE 27

PAGE 31

PAGE 32

PAGE 34
SEE NEXT PAGE FOR MORE STICKERS.

PAGE 34

PAGE 46

PAGE 48

SHOWBABY

INDEPENDENT QUEEN

V.R.Q.T.

SURFER BABE

TREASURE

FRESH

PAGE 53

PAGE 58

MAKING MY DEBUT

PAGE 61

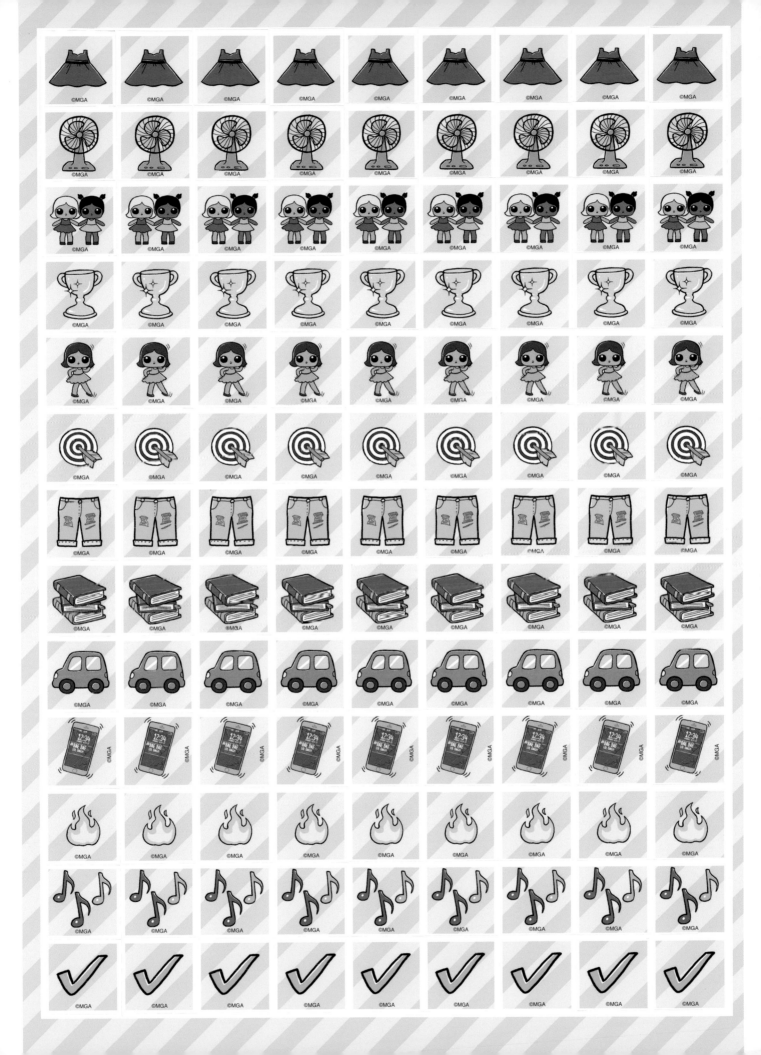

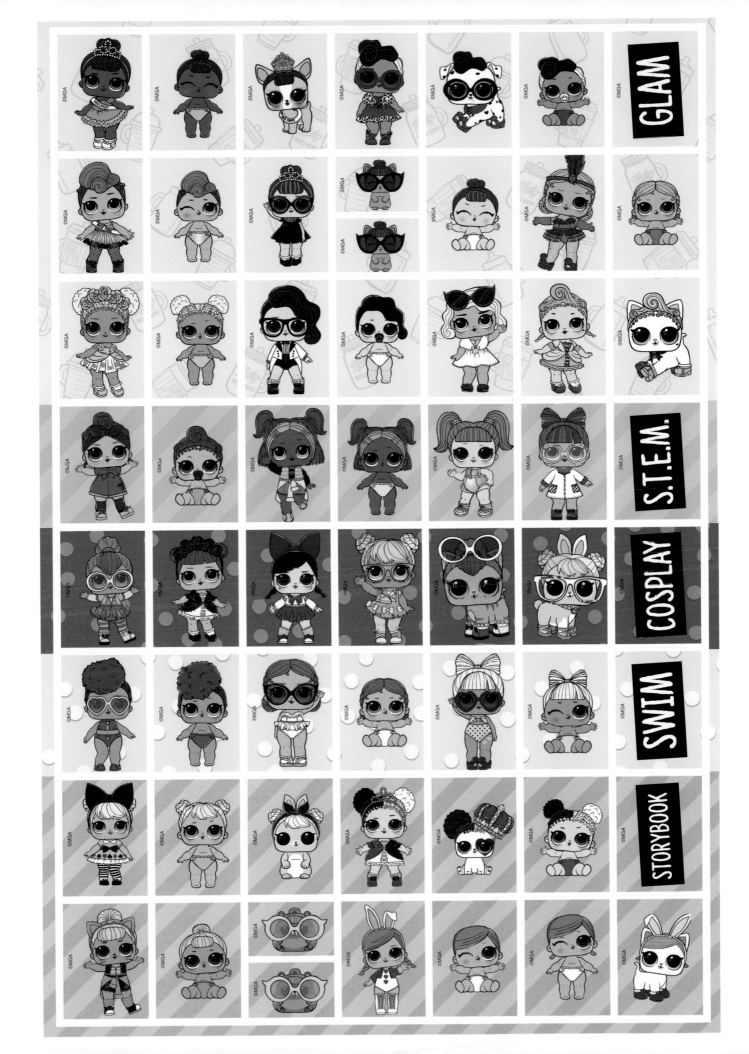

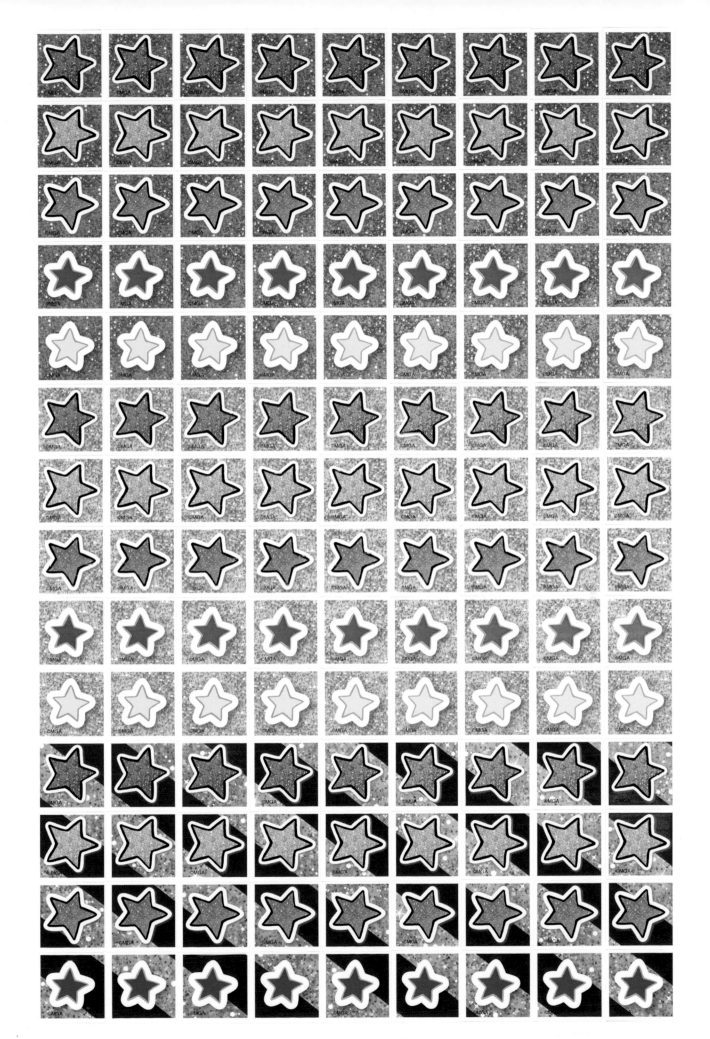

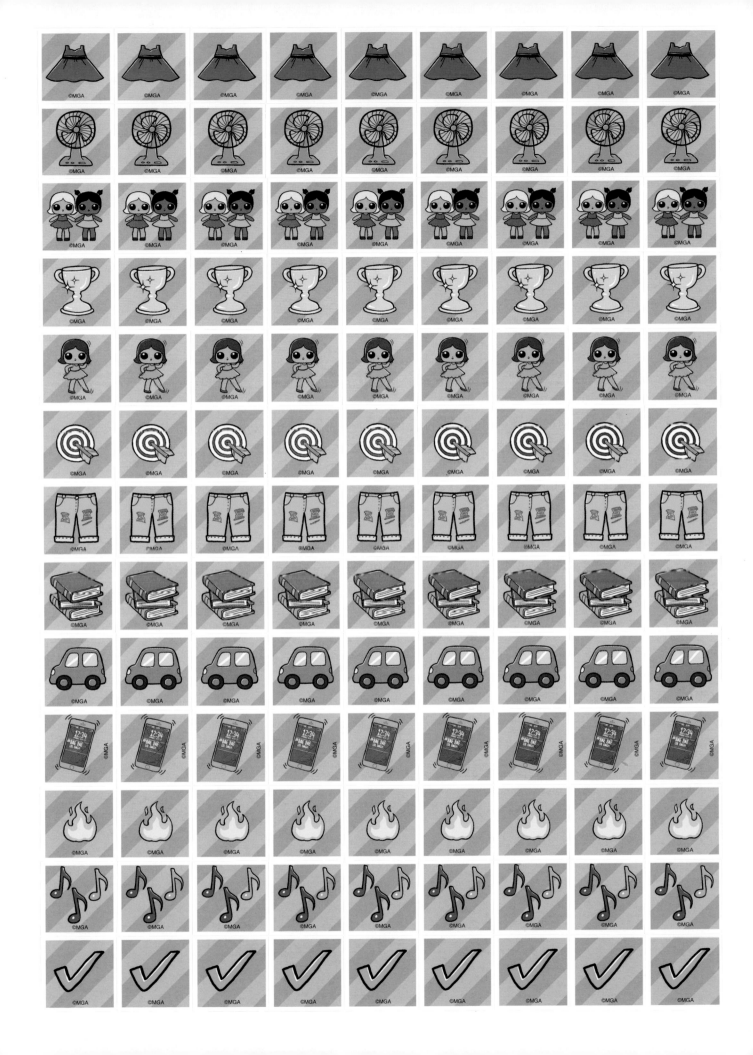

CHILL OUT

ATHLETIC

GLEE

HIP HOP

OPPOSITES

ROCK

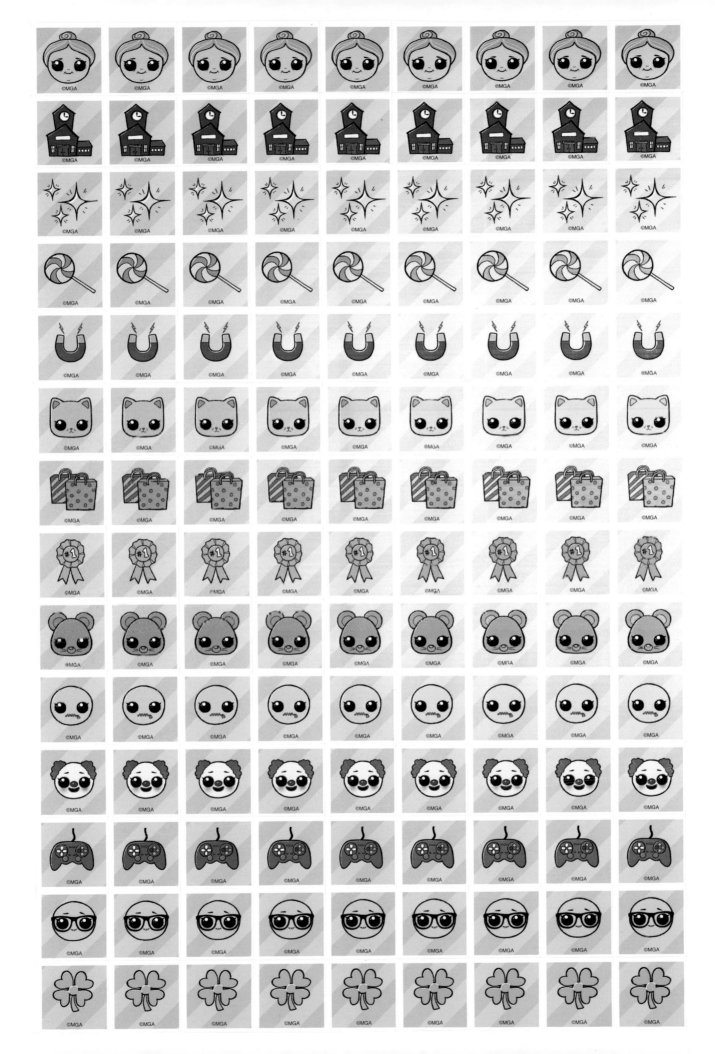

THIS BOOK
BELONGS TO:
_ _ _ _ _ _ _ _ _ _ _ _ _

L.O.L. SURPRISE!: 1000 STICKER BOOK
A CENTUM BOOK 978-1-912396-52-8

L.O.L. SURPRISE! DOLLS COLOUR AND CARRY
A CENTUM BOOK 978-1-912396-53-5

Published in Great Britain by Centum Books Ltd.
This edition published 2020.
1 3 5 7 9 10 8 6 4 2

ISBN 978-1-4998-1082-0

Distributed by

BuzzPop
an imprint of Little Bee Books

251 Park Avenue South, New York, NY 10010
BuzzPop and associated colophon are trademarks of Little Bee Books.
buzzpopbooks.com

For information about special discounts on bulk purchases,
please contact Little Bee Books at sales@littlebeebooks.com.

Centum Books Ltd, 20 Devon Square, Newton Abbot, Devon, TQ12 2HR, UK
books@centumbooksltd.co.uk
CENTUM BOOKS Limited Reg. No. 07641486

Manufactured in China TPL 0420

© MGA

MEOW! WOOF! SQUEAK!

The L.O.L. Surprise! pets are just as cute 'n' sassy as their doll BFFs. Design a new purr-fect pal for the tots to adopt.

DRAW YOUR PET HERE!

DON'T FORGET THEIR AWESOME ACCESSORIES

GIVE THEM A CUTE QUOTE

DESIGN A BEAUT BOTTLE FOR THEM

MOVE TO THE MUSIC

Step to it! Sis Swing can't wait to get groovin'
with her Dance Club cuties. Follow the key across
the colored squares to lead her to them.

KEY 1 2 3 4

YOU CAN GO UP, DOWN,
LEFT OR RIGHT, BUT
NOT DIAGONALLY.

START

FINISH

ANSWER ON PAGE 63

5

© MGA

TEACHER'S PET

Spirit Club

CODE-BREAKIN' BABES

Only a true BFF can decode this message
from the Spirit Club sweeties!
Use the key to reveal what it says.

GIVE ME AN A FOR AWESOME!

IT'S CLASSY TO BE SMART

K	H	A	O	U	E	G

C	M	R	W	Y	B	T

WHEN YOU'VE DECODED THE
MESSAGE, REWARD YOURSELF
WITH A GOLD STAR STICKER.

ANSWER ON PAGE 63

7

© MGA

PRETTY IN PASTEL.

BON BON

Cosplay Club

© MGA

JUST COS-PLAYIN'

Hop Hop needs your help to find her way to Bon Bon. Use your pawprint stickers to create a path through the maze.

START

FINISH

ANSWER ON PAGE 63

9

© MGA

FASHION FIX

The Retro Club gals all have a statement fashion piece which makes them go gaga. Can you work out which doll matches each item? Place the correct sticker on top of each shadow.

A

A PINK LEATHER JACKET

B

GLAMOROUS GO-GO BOOTS

C

A STRIPY SHIRT AND BERET

D

A TOP WITH FABULOUS FRINGING

E

A PERFECTLY POLKA-DOTTED DRESS

ANSWERS ON PAGE 63

11

© MGA

SASS 'N' SMARTS

The S.T.E.M. Club love to discover and invent.
Design a cool new gadget for them to build.

NAME YOUR GADGET: _____

DRAW YOUR GADGET HERE:

LAB IS FAB!

WHAT IS IT USED FOR?

_____
_____
_____
_____

IF IT AIN'T BROKE, DON'T FIX IT!

FAB FRIENDS

What kind of friend are you?
Take this cute quiz to find out.

CHILLIN' WITH MY HOMIES

You and your BFF have a massive falling-out. What do you do?
A. APOLOGIZE IMMEDIATELY. I CAN'T STAY MAD AT THEM FOR LONG ☐
B. GIVE THEM SPACE AND MAKE UP EVENTUALLY ☐
C. DON'T WORRY TOO MUCH. THERE ARE LOADS OF OTHER PEOPLE TO HANG OUT WITH ☐

At school, you spend most of your lunchtime …
A. CHATTING WITH YOUR BFF ☐
B. CHILLING WITH YOUR SQUAD ☐
C. TRYING NEW SCHOOL CLUBS ☐

You're hanging out with your friends on the weekend, which means you'll be …
A. HAVING A SLEEPOVER AND SWAPPING SECRETS ☐
B. GOING SHOPPING ☐ C. GOING TO A PARTY ☐

What's the most important thing about your friends?
A. THEY ALWAYS HAVE MY BACK ☐
B. THEY ACCEPT ME FOR WHO I AM ☐
C. WE KNOW HOW TO HAVE FUN ☐

What do you and your friends have in common?
A. EVERYTHING. THAT'S WHY WE'RE BFFS ☐
B. OUR SENSE OF HUMOR ☐ C. OUR HOBBIES ☐

MOSTLY As
YOU'RE QUITE SELECTIVE ABOUT THE FRIENDS YOU MAKE AND WOULD RATHER HAVE A FEW BEST FRIENDS THAN LOTS OF ACQUAINTANCES. IT CAN TAKE YOU A WHILE TO OPEN UP TO PEOPLE, BUT ONCE YOU DO, YOU'RE FIERCELY LOYAL. YOU ALWAYS SUPPORT YOUR FRIENDS AND WOULD DO ANYTHING TO MAKE THEM HAPPY.

MOSTLY Bs
HAVING A LAUGH WITH YOUR FRIENDS IS THE MOST IMPORTANT THING TO YOU. YOU'D RATHER HANG OUT WITH THEM THAN DO BASICALLY ANYTHING ELSE. IT'S ALL ABOUT #MAKINGMEMORIES. YOU KNOW THAT YOUR FRIENDS WILL ACCEPT YOU NO MATTER WHAT AND YOU'D DO THE SAME FOR THEM – THAT'S WHAT MAKES YOU SO CLOSE!

MOSTLY Cs
YOU'RE A SOCIAL BUTTERFLY, WHO'S FRIENDS WITH PRACTICALLY EVERYONE. FOR YOU, HAVING FRIENDS IS ALL ABOUT HAVING FUN AND YOU LOVE TO BE THE LIFE OF EVERY PARTY. INSTEAD OF HAVING ONE BFF, YOU PREFER HAVING LOTS OF DIFFERENT PEOPLE TO TALK TO AND HANG OUT WITH.

STICKER SURPRISE

The lil rebels love surprises! Match your stickers to the numbered spaces below to reveal a secret image.

ANSWER ON PAGE 63

© MGA

17

ROLLIN' WITH MY HAMMIES

M.C. Hammy and Rolls are racing to the finish, but who will win? Turn the book around and then race a friend. The fastest finisher wins!

START

FINISH

20

© MGA

START

FINISH

21

© MGA

GIMME THAT GLITTER

The Glitterati gurls' outfits are always on point. Design new accessories for these glamorous babes and then use your stickers to decorate them. Shine bright, babies!

WHAT'S THE **BUZZ,** HONEY?

PURR-FECTION!

CLUB CROSSWORD

Each clue below refers to a club – can you figure out what they are? Once you do, fit each name into the crossword. When you're finished, rearrange the letters in the highlighted squares to spell out a surprise word!

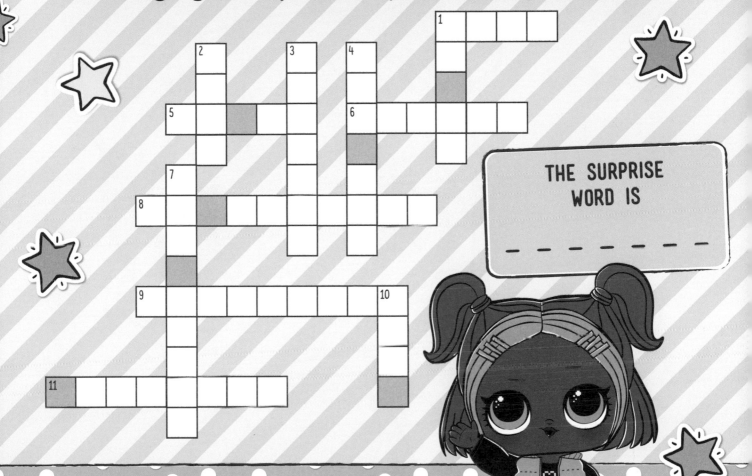

THE SURPRISE WORD IS

_ _ _ _ _ _ _ _

ACROSS
1. THIS CLUB LOVES ROCKIN' OUT TO TOP BANDS.
5. THIS CLUB NEVER MISSES A BEAT!
6. NO ONE HAS MORE SCHOOL SPIRIT THAN THIS GROUP.
8. THESE BABES ARE LIVING THEIR BEST GLITTER LIFE.
9. FOR THIS CLUB, IT'S ALL ABOUT CELEBRATING YOUR DIFFERENCES.
11. THESE SPORTY GIRLS KNOW YOU NEED TO BE IN IT TO WIN IT!

DOWN
1. THESE FASHIONISTAS TAKE INSPIRATION FROM THE PAST.
2. THIS CLUB TAKES THE BEST SELFIES.
3. THESE SWEETIES BELONG ON THE STAGE.
4. THESE B.B.s LOVE TO DRESS UP AS THEIR FAVORITE CHARACTERS.
7. THESE GURLS LOVE SLUMBER PARTIES AND SWAPPING SECRETS.
10. LOOKING COOL BY THE POOL IS WHAT THIS CLUB DOES BEST.

25

ANSWERS ON PAGE 63

BABY CAT

CHECK MEOWT!

Theater Club

26

© MGA

BRAVO BABES

These #showstoppers were born to perform! Can you find eight differences between these two pictures of the Theater Club?

ADD A STICKER EACH TIME YOU SPOT A DIFFERENCE

ANSWERS ON PAGE 63

27

© MGA

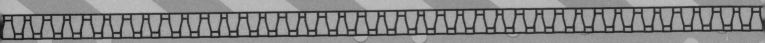

MERBABY

I'D RATHER BE SWIMMING.

Theater Club

28

© MGA

BORN TO BE STARS

The lil rebels are all about living your best life and being whoever you want to be. Fill in these future predictions about you and your fab friends.

The friend most likely to win gold at the Olympics is

- - - - - - - - - - - - - - - - - - - -

They've got serious sports skills.

The friend most likely to become a superstar singer is

- - - - - - - - - - - - - - - - - - - -

Their voice is beautiful.

The friend most likely to become a fashion icon is

- - - - - - - - - - - - - - - - - - - -

They can make anything stylish!

The friend most likely to invent something amazing is

- - - - - - - - - - - - - - - - - - - -

They're supersmart.

The friend most likely to write the next bestseller is

- - - - - - - - - - - - - - - - - - - -

Everything they write is incredible.

The friend most likely to become a stage sensation is

- - - - - - - - - - - - - - - - - - - -

Acting is their passion.

HIDDEN GEMS

Bet ya can't find them all! How many of the L.O.L. Surprise! crew can you see in this picture? As you spot each character, add a heart sticker next to their picture.

CAN YOU SPOT ...

A   B   C   D   E

CAN YOU NAME ALL THE OTHER CHARACTERS IN THIS SNAP?

ANSWERS ON PAGE 63

31

© MGA

DIVING DIVAS

The Swim Club took a cute vacay selfie together, but it got wet! Place your stickers in the right order to reassemble their picture. #staycoolatthepool

32

ANSWER ON PAGE 64

© MGA

ALL THE ANIMALS

The lil rockers are smitten with their paw-fect pets.
Use your stickers to match the correct doll
to their a-meow-zing mate.

A

B

C

D

E

F

© MGA

WHICH L.O.L. SURPRISE!
PET IS YOUR FAVE?

ALL TOGETHER NOW

The Athletic Club knows you have to be in it to win it! These girls give their all on the field, court, track and everywhere else. Design a cool clubhouse where they can hang out as one big team.

YOU BETTA NOT DROP THE BALL

TOUCHDOWN

BABY BOWL CHAMPION!

Athletic Club

© MGA

TIME TO SHINE!

For Crystal Queen, life is better with bling!
Color in the shapes with
dots inside to reveal her BFF.

PSST! THE ANSWER
IS ALSO HER QUOTE.

_ _ _ _ _ _ _
ARE MY BFF

ANSWER ON PAGE 64

© MGA

CRYSTAL QUEEN

Glitterati

© MGA

BANGIN' BEATS

It's all about jammin' to your favorite tunes and singin' your heart out with the Rock Club. Pick one of the members and design an awesome new outfit for them. Rock out!

BUILD A BFF

The L.O.L. Surprise! dolls love making friends.
Create a brand-new BFF for the lil rockers
to chill out with.

NAME: _____

WHICH CLUB WILL THEY BELONG TO? CHECK ONE BOX BELOW OR MAKE UP A NEW CLUB.

- [ ] 24K GOLD
- [ ] THE GLITTERATI
- [ ] ATHLETIC
- [ ] CHILL OUT
- [ ] COSPLAY
- [ ] DANCE
- [ ] GLAM
- [ ] GLEE
- [ ] HIP HOP
- [ ] OPPOSITES
- [ ] RETRO
- [ ] ROCK
- [ ] SLEEPOVER
- [ ] SPIRIT
- [ ] S.T.E.M.
- [ ] STORYBOOK
- [ ] SWIM
- [ ] THEATER
- [ ] _____

DRAW A PICTURE OF YOUR DOLL HERE!

GIVE THEM A CUTE QUOTE.

DRAW THEIR FIERCE ACCESSORIES.

DIFFERENT IN ALL THE RIGHT WAYS!

Now take a look at the doll you've created and design their opposite.

NAME: _____

WHICH CLUB WILL THEY BELONG TO? CHECK ONE BOX BELOW OR MAKE UP A NEW CLUB.

- [ ] 24K GOLD
- [ ] THE GLITTERATI
- [ ] ATHLETIC
- [ ] CHILL OUT
- [ ] COSPLAY
- [ ] DANCE
- [ ] GLAM
- [ ] GLEE
- [ ] HIP HOP
- [ ] OPPOSITES
- [ ] RETRO
- [ ] ROCK
- [ ] SLEEPOVER
- [ ] SPIRIT
- [ ] S.T.E.M.
- [ ] STORYBOOK
- [ ] SWIM
- [ ] THEATER
- [ ] _____

GIVE THEM A COOL QUOTE.

DRAW A PICTURE OF YOUR DOLL HERE!

DON'T FORGET THEIR AWESOME ACCESSORIES.

MIC DROP

Nothing makes the Glee Club happier than performing! Use the empty lines below to spit some rhymes and write their next big hit.

CUTE CLOSE-UPS

Can you work out which close-up belongs to which baby?
Place stickers of the lil rebels' names under the close-ups,
and then add their full-length stickers alongside.

A

B

C

D

E

F

© MGA

ANSWERS ON PAGE 64

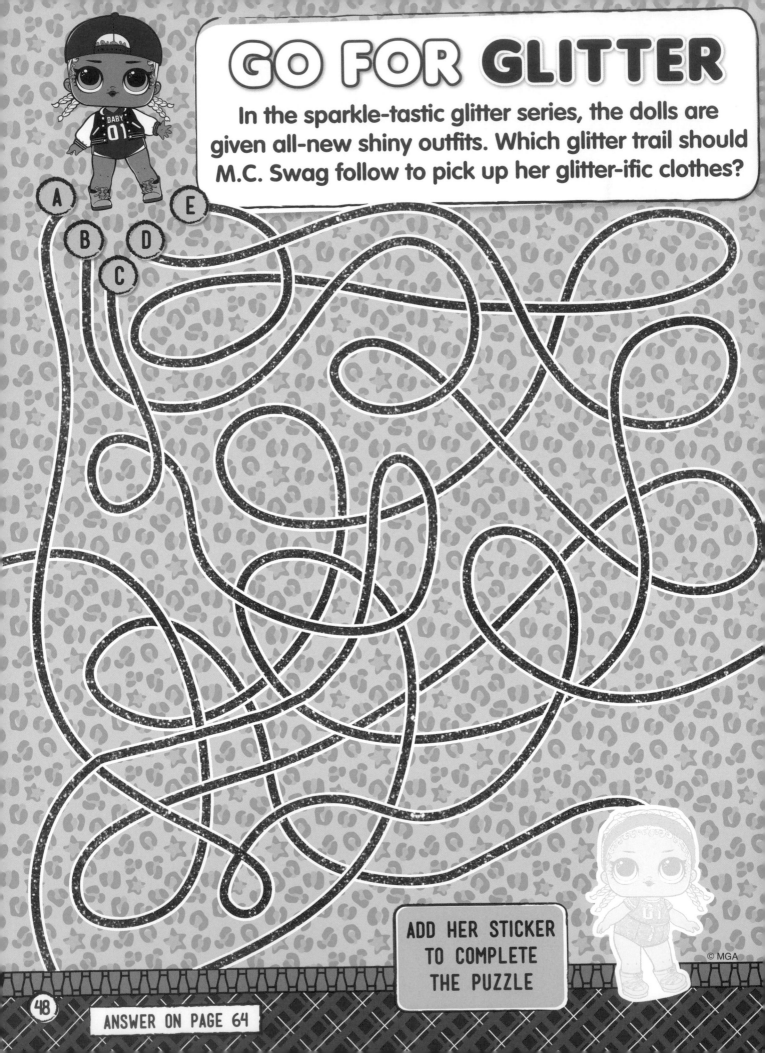

GO FOR GLITTER

In the sparkle-tastic glitter series, the dolls are given all-new shiny outfits. Which glitter trail should M.C. Swag follow to pick up her glitter-ific clothes?

BABY 01

A
B
C
D
E

ADD HER STICKER
TO COMPLETE
THE PUZZLE

© MGA

ANSWER ON PAGE 64

ANIMAL LOVER

The L.O.L. Surprise! dolls each have their own fur-ever friend, but who's yours? Answer these questions to find out!

Pick a color:
A. PINK ☐   B. ORANGE ☐
C. BLUE ☐   D. PURPLE ☐

Which accessory would you rock?
A. GLASSES ☐   B. BOW ☐
C. HEADBAND ☐   D. SCARF ☐

What would you prefer to do?
A. HANG OUT WITH FRIENDS ☐
B. SNUGGLE UP WITH A BOOK ☐
C. GO FOR A WALK OR PLAY A GAME ☐
D. TRY A NEW ACTIVITY ☐

What do you value most in a best friend?
A. GOOD SENSE OF HUMOR ☐
B. LOYALTY ☐   C. FUN ☐   D. HONESTY ☐

Choose a treat:
A. COOKIES ☐   B. CAKE ☐
C. PIZZA ☐   D. ICE CREAM ☐

MOSTLY As – CHERRY HAM
YOU SEE CHERRY HAM ROLLIN', YOU LOVIN'! JUST LIKE CHERRY HAM, YOU'RE EASILY EXCITABLE AND ALWAYS HAVE BUNDLES OF ENERGY. YOUR FRIENDS LOVE HANGING OUT WITH YOU BECAUSE THEY KNOW IT'S GOING TO BE A LAUGH.

MOSTLY Bs – COTTONTAIL Q.T.
YOU'RE A LITTLE SHY LIKE COTTONTAIL Q.T. BUT YOU'RE ALWAYS LOYAL TO YOUR FRIENDS AND STAND BY THEM NO MATTER WHAT. YOUR FAVE THING TO DO IS SNUGGLE UNDER A BLANKET WITH A GOOD BOOK - FINGERS CROSSED IT'LL BE A HOPPY ENDING!

MOSTLY Cs – HOOPS D.O.G.G.
IT'S PUPPY LOVE AT FIRST SIGHT! FOR YOU AND HOOPS D.O.G.G., THERE'S NOTHING BETTER THAN BEING OUTSIDE - WHETHER THAT'S GOING ON A WALK OR PLAYING A GAME WITH FRIENDS. YOU ALWAYS GIVE 100% AND APPROACH THINGS WITH THE CONFIDENCE THAT YOU'RE GOING TO WIN.

MOSTLY Ds – SU-PURR KITTY
YOU AND SU-PURR KITTY ARE THE PURR-FECT PAIR. BOTH OF YOU ARE INDEPENDENT, ADVENTUROUS AND BRAVE - READY TO TAKE ON ANY CHALLENGES THAT COME YOUR WAY. YOU LOVE TRYING NEW THINGS AND BEING PUSHED OUT OF YOUR COMFORT ZONE.

SLEEPOVER SECRETS

This outrageous game will have you and your BFFs giggling all night. Take turns asking each other one of the questions below, starting each one with "Would you rather..."

ANSWER A TRUTH **OR** TAKE A DARE?

GO TO THE MOON **OR** THE BOTTOM OF THE SEA?

NEVER BE ABLE TO EAT YOUR FAVORITE FOOD AGAIN **OR** ONLY EAT YOUR FAVORITE FOOD FOREVER?

JUMP IN A POOL OF MUD **OR** CHOCOLATE ICE CREAM?

HAVE TO DANCE EVERYWHERE INSTEAD OF WALKING **OR** SING INSTEAD OF TALKING?

BE REALLY HOT **OR** REALLY COLD?

BE A DOG **OR** A CAT?

TIME TRAVEL ANYWHERE IN THE FUTURE **OR** ANYWHERE IN THE PAST?

WHEN YOU'VE FINISHED WITH THESE, MAKE UP YOUR OWN!

BE REALLY SHORT **OR** REALLY TALL?

HAVE OVERLY LARGE HANDS **OR** VERY SMALL FEET?

52

STICK-TAC-TOE

Play this glamorous game with your best bae.

HOW TO PLAY:

1. EACH PLAYER CHOOSES AN ICON STICKER.
2. TAKE TURNS PLACING YOUR STICKERS INTO THE GRID.
3. THE FIRST ONE TO GET **THREE IN A ROW** WINS!

DO U KNOW ME?

Challenge your BFF to this quiz and see if you really know each other as well as you think! Put the book between you, then both fill in your answers – no peeking! When you've finished, check your answers with each other and see how you've done.

ABOUT YOU   ABOUT THEM

1. WHO'S YOUR FAVE L.O.L. SURPRISE! DOLL?

2. WHAT TALENT WOULD YOU MOST LIKE TO HAVE?

3. IF YOU COULD GO ANYWHERE IN THE WORLD, WHERE WOULD IT BE?

4. WHAT'S YOUR FAVORITE ANIMAL?

5. WHICH L.O.L. SURPRISE! CLUB IS PERFECT FOR YOU?

6. WHAT'S YOUR FAVORITE FOOD?

ABOUT YOU   ABOUT THEM

1. WHO'S YOUR FAVE L.O.L. SURPRISE! DOLL?

- - - - - - - - - - - - - - - - - - - -

2. WHAT TALENT WOULD YOU MOST LIKE TO HAVE?

- - - - - - - - - - - - - - - - - - - -

3. IF YOU COULD GO ANYWHERE IN THE WORLD, WHERE WOULD IT BE?

- - - - - - - - - - - - - - - - - - - -

4. WHAT'S YOUR FAVORITE ANIMAL?

- - - - - - - - - - - - - - - - - - - -

5. WHICH L.O.L. SURPRISE! CLUB IS PERFECT FOR YOU?

- - - - - - - - - - - - - - - - - - - -

6. WHAT'S YOUR FAVORITE FOOD?

- - - - - - - - - - - - - - - - - - - -

57

© MGA

GOT SELFIE GAME?

Can anyone take a better selfie than the Glam Club? Stick in or draw a picture of you and your BFFs taking your best selfie. Then use your stickers to decorate the frame and photo.

ONCE UPON A ...

It's story time! Fill in the blanks to finish these tales.
You can make them as silly or as fabulous as you like.

THERE WAS ONCE A _____ WHO REALLY WISHED THEY COULD

_____. SO THEY WENT TO SEE _____, WHO TOLD THEM

IF THEY WANTED TO FULFILL THEIR DREAMS, THEY WOULD NEED TO _____.

A BRAND-NEW DISCOVERY HAS BEEN MADE! SCIENTISTS HAVE FOUND _____

LIVING _____. THEY ARE _____ AND _____.

THE STRANGEST THING IS THAT THEY ONLY SEEM TO EAT ONE THING, WHICH IS

_____.

AN ASTRONAUT WAS HURTLING THROUGH SPACE, WHEN SUDDENLY THEY SAW

_____ OUT OF THE WINDOW. THEY COULDN'T BELIEVE THEIR EYES!

THEY DECIDED TO _____ SO THAT THEY COULD _____.

A TIME TRAVELER ARRIVED IN _____. ALL AROUND THEM, THEY SAW

_____ AND _____. IT LOOKED DIFFERENT FROM THE

PRESENT DAY BECAUSE _____, BUT THE ONE THING THAT REMAINED

THE SAME WAS _____.

CURIOUS Q.T.

NEW WORLD. WHO DIS?

Storybook Club

© MGA

WHAT'S NEXT, B.B.?

Almost there! Can you work out what comes next in each sequence? Use your stickers to complete the rows.

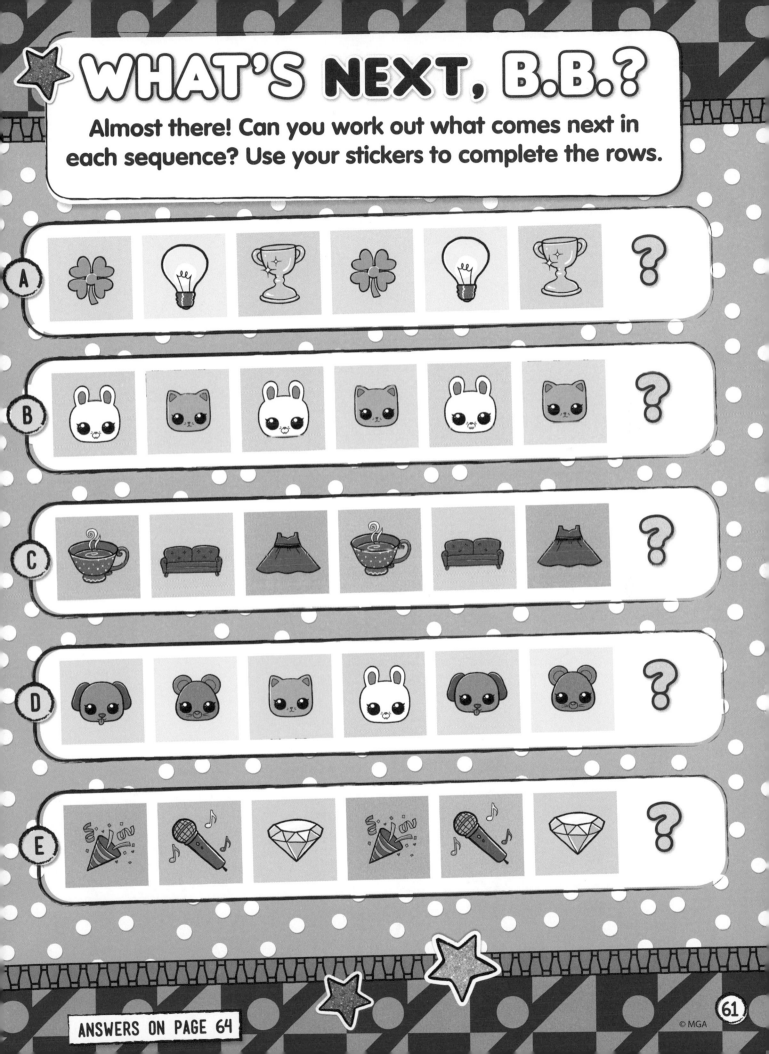

© MGA

JOIN THE CLUB

Follow the trails and write down each letter you pass to reveal which club each tot belongs to. #squadgoals

COURT CHAMP BELONGS TO THE _ _ _ _ _ CLUB.

SLEEPY BONES BELONGS TO THE _ _ _ _ _ CLUB.

MERBABY BELONGS TO THE _ _ _ _ _ CLUB.

GLITTER QUEEN BELONGS TO THE

© MGA

ANSWERS ON PAGE 64

PAGE 5

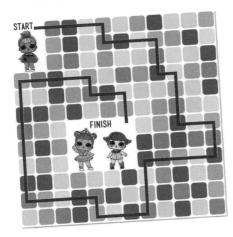

PAGE 7

The message says:
Hey momma! We got ur back.

PAGE 9

PAGE 11

A. PINK BABY
B. GO-GO GURL
C. BEATNIK BABE
D. FOXY
E. JITTERBUG

PAGE 17

PAGES 20-21

PAGE 25

ACROSS: 1. ROCK, 5. DANCE,
6. SPIRIT, 8. GLITTERATI, 9. OPPOSITES,
11. ATHLETIC
DOWN: 1. RETRO, 2. GLAM, 3. THEATER,
4. COSPLAY, 7. SLEEPOVER, 10. SWIM
The surprise word is: NAPTIME

PAGE 27

PAGE 31

PAGE 32

PAGE 34

PAGE 38

DIAMONDS are Crystal Queen's BFF.

PAGE 46

A - Independent Queen

B - Showbaby

C - Fresh

D - Surfer Babe

E - Treasure

F - V.R.Q.T.

PAGE 48

Path E

PAGE 61

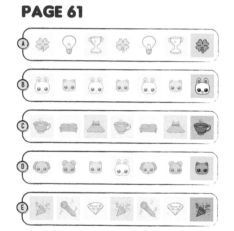

PAGE 62

Court Champ belongs to the **ATHLETIC** Club.

Sleepy Bones belongs to the **SLEEPOVER** Club.

Merbaby belongs to the **THEATER** Club.

Glitter Queen belongs to the **GLITTERATI**.